Nemesis[1]

A Good Guide for Bad Guys

Being an Exceedingly Practical Manual to Achieving Eminence as an Archenemy, Villain, Evil Overlord, & Antihero[2]

Joseph J. Bailey[4]
Underhenchman

<u>*Read this if you value your life*</u>:

1. *Presented for your reading displeasure.*
2. *This means you![3]*
3. *Now pay attention.*
4. *As originally cataloged by the infamous Saedeus Moerdencanum, warlock, dictator, despot, and all-around not so nice guy.*

Read this if you value your life:

1. *A villain must be astute enough to recognize truth from falsehood and fiction from reality.*

Author's Note:[1]

This brief, rather vainglorious treatise is intended for ne'er-do-wells who aspire to more than the abject misery and failure that has been their continued, overwhelming, and unremitting lot in life despite their most earnest efforts and grandest visions.

Herein you will find the keys to unlock success in the kingdom of evil.[2]

You're welcome.

Read this if you value your life:

1. *This book is written all in good (or evil) fun. If you do not like good (or evil), then this book is not for you.*
2. *And by this I mean the vast realm of self-interest, particularly your own.*

Nemesis's Note:

For those who are nemeses, this tome will remain unencoded, intelligible, and trap-free.

For non-nemeses, including most lazy uninspired wastrels hoping to become nemeses, this treatise will appear to be an obtuse, overly symbolic thesis on the many virtues of attempting to solve insoluble puzzles, conundrums, and problems under the strict time constraints imposed by a wide array of life-threatening traps and devices.[1]

Read this if you value your life:

1. *For those particularly persistent but bromidic this tome will transform into one such especially menacing contrivance.[2]*
2. *You have been warned.*

To those who laugh,
but, more importantly, to those who share joy (or evil) with others

Being a villain is fraught with unending challenges and mind-shattering difficulties.

It is also quite fun.

Your rewards will be commensurate with your efforts (and the numbers of enemies you crush beneath your heel).

- Djazoth Al'Zann
World-conquering antihero, cultivator of rare orchids, and collector of stuffed bunnies

Do not fear Darkness for It is merely the absence of Light.

- Shen Po
Master of the void palm, one of the fallen founding fathers of the K'un Lun, member of the Cabal, striker of poses, and stylish connoisseur of fine robes

Table of Contents

The Villainy of Villainy

You are a villain—the bane of countless, a scourge to your foes, a desecrator of the commonplace, a breaker of boundaries, and a destroyer of the accepted.

Innumerable are the faults and blames laid upon you.

Myriad are the travesties heaped upon your character.[1]

The burdens and failings of many are thrown upon you as though these weaknesses were your own.[2]

The true crime of being a villain is not to be found in the offenses you commit, the wanton acts you undertake, or the sacrileges you pronounce.[3]

No, the true crime in being a villain lies not in the actions undertaken by you.

Rather, the true villainy of being a villain falls at the feet of those around you.

The true villains are:

Those who would deny you your freedom.

Those who would limit your choice.

Those who would prohibit you from acting in your own interest.

Those who view their way as the right or only approach at the expense of yours and others'.

The true villains are not those who would act of their own accord.

The true villains are not those who act in their own self-interest.

The true villains are those who would prevent you from doing as you would.[5]

Read this if you value your life:

9

1. *Granted, a scant few may have some ever so slight modicum of justification.*
2. *In truth, you merely profit from them.*
3. *Although these may be a good place to start.*[4]
4. *Especially for the shortsighted and other fools of limited vision.*
5. *Now do your best not to get caught.*

How Evil is *Evil?*

Evil is a spectrum.[1]

The spectrum of evil is one gauged by selfishness. Being evil, then, is a matter of degree, the expression of that selfishness the cause.

From a societal standpoint, and according to the more common misapprehensions of the misguided: the more selfish your actions, the greater your intrinsic "evilness."

I don't like spectrums just as I don't particularly care for rainbows.

The most altruistic, compassionate individual or group does what they must, what they deem to be just, that which they have judged to be correct.

You are no different.

You just happen to put your interests before those of others, and aren't afraid of stepping on some toes along the way.

I call this evility.
Unlike civility, evility is the expression of the individual's needs and interests before the needs of the group—or, alternately, the expression of one group's needs ahead of another's.

Evility is often about survivability.

If evil is measured along a spectrum, then your spectrum burns.[2]

Read this if you value your life:

1. *And I'm not talking about color.*
2. *This is, in fact, the reason why many "evil" individuals often wear sunglasses at inappropriate times. We just burn a bit brighter than most.*

Some Positives

I don't like being positive[1], so I will keep this brief.

Being a reprobate does have its perks.

As an evildoer:

You don't have to say you're sorry.
Ever.

You don't have to show mercy.
Most especially when someone shrieks, "Uncle!"[5]

You don't have to worry about what people think of or about you.
What effect could someone else's thoughts or opinions possibly have on your well-being if they don't matter in the first place?
Worrying about social faux pas is a thing of the past!

You can always speak your mind.
Particularly when doing so makes you feel better at the expense of others.[6]

You don't owe anyone anything.
And you determine the terms when and if you pay.[7]

You can keep things simple.
To this end, I employ a simple question-and-answer system when evaluating a relationship:

> Is this person helping me achieve a desired end?
>   1. If yes, then keep them around a while longer.
>   2. If no, eliminate them.[8]

You answer to no one.
Unless of course you're interrogating someone… then you may deign to communicate if it helps to extract the necessary information from the urchin in question.

The only limits you have are those defined by yourself.

Be a villain.

There's nothing better.[9]

Read this if you value your life:

1. *Except when I want to be certain, explicit, emphatic, without question, and confident.*[2]
2. *Which is basically all the time but that's a different kind of positivity.*[3]
3. *The kind I do like.*[4]
4. *Now wipe that smile off your face.*
5. *Even if you are their uncle.*
6. *You benefit twice!*
7. *And I'm notoriously cheap.*
8. *Remember, no one's time, interests, or motivations are more valuable than your own.*
9. *By that I don't mean good.*

Choosing a Proper Nom de Guerre

Do you think I was born with the name Saedeus?

How naïve are you?

No.

My given name is Thom.[1]

In a world with dragons, warlocks, daemons, necromancers, and undead, do you think I could go by the name of Thom and command any respect?

How many Dark Lords do you know with a name like mine?

Thom the Merciless?

Thom the Mighty?

Thom the Fell?

Evil Overlord Thom… Give me a break!

I don't think so.

The sooner you adopt a more suitable name, one that reflects your nature and intentions, the fewer people you'll have to eliminate.

Also, the less taunting you'll have to endure.

Read this if you value your life:

1. *You think I'm going to give YOU my true name? I have enough problems as it is!*

14

Titles and Honorifics

As important as selecting a suitable nom de guerre is to making a lasting impression and determining your long-term success as a destroyer of others' hopes and dreams, just as critical is choosing an appropriate title or honorific.

Your appellation should reflect your character, your persona, and the oppressive emotions you would inflict upon others.[1]

Are you a knight of destruction?

How would you like to be recognized by the common lot of Men, Orcs, Dwarves, and Gnomes?

How about with the less common lot of Yerens, Dracodaerans, Indural, Aeryn D'al, H'era, Jira S'al Alann, Nüaer'Daer, Anubaraëthi, Anubavaeri, and the like?

Although Black Knight and Dark Knight are acceptable[2], why not add another layer of menace with Dread Lord, Blade of Woe, or Umbral Lord?

Alternatively, why not throw your rivals off entirely with something in the vein of Master of Severed Arms or Fell Knight of the Blunted Blade?[3]

Are you the head of a cult?

Although Priest of the Unholy Rites has a certain ring, why not add an honorific reflective of your cult's intent, one that is easily understood, while carrying the requisite underlying menace?

Perhaps Soul Reaper, Tyrant of the Unclean, Maw of Darkness, Archon of Putrefaction, or Corrupter of Innocents will suffice as a conversation starter?[4]

If you enjoy a bit of dark humor, why not a title akin to Defiler of the Unwashed or Despoiler of the Unkempt?[5]

Are you a vigilante?

Something fear-inducing and uniquely distinctive while being cringingly memorable should be your target.

How about Shadow Slayer, Abyssborn, Scythe of Darkness, or the Garrote?

If those are a bit too generically pretentious, get creative with an honorific that is entirely unique.

The Shadow Squirrel, Iron Octopus, or Flayer of Bloodthirsty Bunnies will instill a healthy sense of... well, if you can't laugh at yourself, who can?[6]

You are in control of your destiny.[7]
The proper title is an important step to making your future a reality.[8] Do not disappoint!

Read this if you value your life:

1. *Think of your designation as a gift you give to your foes—one they don't especially want but which they will come to appreciate as you inflict its import upon them... repeatedly.*
2. *And quite common... which you are not.*
3. *Okay, maybe not.*
4. *If those titles are too wordy, simple also works. Single-word descriptors can be just as effective as many.*
5. *Let your own incomparable wit shine.*
6. *Or, to be more precise, who can you let laugh at you without having to eliminate them?*
7. *In fact, you are probably in control of many others' destinies, but I digress.*
8. *Or you can just choose a pet designation for yourself and keep the matter entirely private, letting others make of you what they will... the choice is yours.*

Naming Your Weapon

Everything important has a name.[1]

Of utmost importance to you are your chosen weapon(s).

Often, the storied weapon(s) you use will already have a name when you strip them from their rightful owner.
Sometimes, their names will evolve as you inflict terror and heartbreak on your victims.
At other times, a name will come to you—perhaps in the moment of the item's creation, or during a particularly baleful deed.
However, having a name in mind for your implement of destruction can put you ahead of the game in terms of generating fear, confusion, chaos, and servility.[2]

Some potential classic names include, but are hardly limited to: The Disemboweler, Fellblade, Shadow's Edge, Night, Fool's Bane, Doomhammer, The Hatchet, Reaper, and the ever-popular Soul Tickler.[3]

Think about what effects you would like your weapon to have upon your enemies physically and psychologically.

Come to terms with the essence of your weapon and let it speak to you.

Then name it appropriately.

Choose wisely.

The world awaits your decision.

Read this if you value your life:

1. *You, being of principal significance, have the most important name of all.*

17

2. *And isn't that what we all want?*
3. *Your mileage will vary... especially depending on your sense of humor and what you can pull off.*

How to Keep Your Secret Plans Secret

Keep your mouth shut![1]

No bragging about the overwhelming greatness of your achievements.

No gloating over fallen rivals or soon-to-be finished adversaries.

No trusting the inner workings of your mind with close accomplices, hirelings, or allies.

No broadcasting of the unfolding of your latest (or earliest) plans.

I know this is tough!

It's hard enough being a self-important egomaniac as it is without trying to keep everything locked up inside.

After all, the world begs to listen to our greatness.

But do it!

You'll thank me.[2]

Whenever your input is required or suggested in (im)polite conversation, practice your most menacing expression, your dourest glare, your most distant stoic gaze of untouchable aloofness, your most inviolable regard of irreproachable condescension, or whatever baleful visage suits your mood or style.

Making faces can be fun.

Clouding your words and actions in an impenetrable haze of obfuscation and misdirection is one of the hallmarks of our craft.

Losing everything you have worked so diligently for in your life because you cannot hold your tongue… not so much.

Read this if you value your life:

1. _Or whatever equivalent you may have._
2. _Well, a normal person would. From you, I expect nothing._

On Stupidity (Particularly of Others)

There are few irrefutable laws of the macroverse.

Principal among these axioms is that people[1] are stupid.

Throughout your conquests, triumphs, and victories, you will be amazed at the breadth and depth of the idiocy of sentient[2] beings.

Let this asininity be a source of humor, and as an inspiration for your continued prosperity and purpose in the greater multiverse, but never doubt it.

Make yourself the exception.

Lest you die.[3]

Read this if you value your life:

1. *And their equivalents.*
2. *I use this term loosely.*
3. *No better or different from all the rest.*

Recruitment Policies

Do you wish to excel in villainy?[1]

Then you must set your standards high and adhere to them.[3]

Do not give in to short-term vagaries or whims. You must plan for the long-term and act accordingly.

Of paramount importance in achieving these ends is surrounding yourself with the right accomplices, hirelings, henchmen, underlings, allies, consorts, and associates.

Ever aim for competence and quality.

Some points to consider and/or avoid:

1. Friends of friends – Are generally to be avoided. The last thing you want is underqualified henchman crowding your ranks. Plus, including the friends of your friends[4] in your legions may complicate already strained relationships.
2. Relations – Haven't you spent enough time with these people already? Aren't they part of the reason you are now a malevolent overlord?[5]
3. Stuttering spellcasters – The last thing you need is one of your wizards unleashing their evil upon you.
4. Blind or maimed archers or marksmen – You want your henchman to strike into the very heart of your foes, not strike you, or hardly strike at all.
5. Zombies, skeletons and automatons – Expecting mindless creatures or devices to be able to perform complex tasks or react to changing conditions is a sure means to countless episodes of frustration.[6]
6. Mercenaries – Although potentially well-disciplined and fearsome in combat, do not expect loyalty from those bought with coin—for someone may always offer more.[7]
7. Overly ambitious employees – You need to use others to be the vehicle for your success. You must avoid being used.

8. Exceptionally intelligent minions – These underlings may quickly comprehend that you are unnecessary… before they have been shown the reverse.
9. Allied groups and individuals – Employing those with pre-existing allegiances to one another risks them banding together to put their interests above your own. This must *never* happen.
10. Egotists – You must always put your concerns first and avoid those who would do otherwise.

You must set your expectations high, that your minions must reach to achieve them. You must choose wisely those who follow you, that they will be able to meet these expectations.

If you do not, I advise cultivating a good sense of humor that you may laugh at the cascading torrents of failure that will wash over you.

I would counsel you to trust your heart, to believe in your conscience, but you are evil. It is in your nature to betray—even yourself.

Sometimes working alone is so much easier… but then so much less gets accomplished.

Read this if you value your life:

1. *If you are not prepared to excel in evil, then you must make your peace with hardship, failure, and never-ending threats of impending death.[2]*
2. *Sign me up!*
3. *You may set your standards low, but then you risk becoming a victim like those you would exploit. Where's the fun in that?*
4. *Assuming you have any.*
5. *Also, do you really want to hear about how you weren't so evil or all-powerful as a child? If you do, then by all means hire your uncle.*
6. *But you may get a laugh… especially at yourself.*

7. *This caveat applies equally to anyone you buy or attempt to pay off.*

Kill People with Kindness (After You've Killed the Right Ones)

So… you have decimated entire regions, ransacked cultural and intellectual monuments, waged war on individuals, nations, and world-spanning hegemonies, drained immeasurable potentially irreplaceable resources, and crushed the hopes and dreams of entire generations.[1]

After all this, do you want to maintain your position of power?
Of course!

Do you want to continue to strengthen your empire and expand it beyond its current bounds?
Most assuredly!

Do you want to increase your wealth, status, and personal position?
Certainly!

Do you want to continue to succeed, most especially where other evil overlords have failed?
Absolutely!

Obviously, a few[2] had to be sacrificed along the way to achieve your greater desired ends.

There may also be a need for further similar measures in the future.

However, once you have reorganized, optimized, and repositioned your empire, populace, or organization to your liking, the time has come to maintain and improve upon what you have already labored so mightily to create.

What's next?

Do the unexpected!

Try being nice!

Sure, some atrocities cannot be forgiven, but for those of your subjects that you have not yet eliminated, you may engender enough sense of well-being and appreciation that your efforts at world, galactic, or universal domination may proceed forward unabated.[3]

So kill the survivors with kindness.

You just might be surprised at the results.[4]

Read this if you value your life:

1. *And worse.*
2. *Or many.*
3. *Also, it might just throw your enemies off balance… especially if you do a complete turnaround after gaining power.*
4. *Besides, there's always the option to revert to your old ways should the results not be to your liking.*

How to Be Thankful for What You've Got (I Know It's Hard)

I know too many fellow evildoers who have fallen because they overreached.[1]

Ambition is important, don't get me wrong.

Ambition is the spark that lights your eyes and pushes you ever forward to greater and greater accomplishments.

But ambition can also be your undoing.

Do not reach too far without proper preparation and planning.

You might fall to a coup d'état, be overthrown, miss an important weakness, fail to stabilize your base, or make yourself vulnerable through improper preparation.

Do not push too quickly without the necessary groundwork, support, and fortification.

Your efforts may crumble beneath you, you may fall to an assassin's noose, your lands may revolt in your absence, or your power may wane when spread too thin.

Do not rush forward headlong after opportunity.

You may take on a foe before you are ready, you may miss an important stratagem or opening, you may lose sight of or miss a long-term prospect, or you may fall prey to unexpected surprises or ambushes.

Sometimes it's nice to be thankful for what you have.

Then you can reach for more when you're ready, or the time is right.[2]

And let your desires come to you.[3]

Read this if you value your life:

1. *And I am not talking about overextending themselves at the dinner table, although that does happen to the best of us.*
2. *By waiting, you may also be more likely to be in a position to achieve your aims and savor your reward when you attain it.*
3. *Of course, striking first and hard also has its place. But you would not be where you are without knowing that truism.*

Avoiding Tunnel Vision

You are focused.

You are relentless.

The unflagging fires of your vision and will coalesce into blazing arcs of incandescent power burning forward to the future you crave, allowing you to carve out your conception.

Your supreme concentration can just as easily be your end.

Broaden your view.

Expand your perspective.

Consider the assessments of others.[1]

Do not overlook potential dangers in your pursuit of conquest.

Employ other eyes that you may avoid potential pitfalls and overcome your own weaknesses.[2]

Do not let your unrelenting attention blind you to potential errors and oversights.

Your enemies will not be blind to your failings. Your blunders are their strengths.

Do not let your foes take advantage of your shortcomings.

Often what you can't see will be your undoing.

Open your eyes that you may live![3]

Read this if you value your life:

28

1. *Just because you consider does not mean you have to follow. You are the overlord and you dictate action.*
2. *Not that you have many.*
3. *Just not too wide—the last thing you need is a bug in your eye... then you'll risk being blind... which is arguably worse than tunnel vision.*

Remember to Lock Your Doors

How many times have you gone to visit one of your partners in crime, another nefarious malefactor, or a wretched villain, only to find their lair ransacked, their horde taken, their home despoiled, and your acquaintance either imprisoned or killed?

How often was this unfortunate fall caused by someone forgetting to properly secure their fastness, overlooking the necessity to bar every way in, or otherwise miss that their hold was anything but secure?

Almost always!

Let me make this clear to you now.

Always lock your doors, gates, and portals!

Always secure all the entrances to your keep from the sewer canals!

Always bar all the wells and waterways leading into and out of your castle!

Seal all secret passageways! Uncover and lock any that you may not yet have found!

Do not leave windows ajar or unbarred!

Unused airlocks should never be completely abandoned!

Airducts and ventilation shafts are enemy superhighways! If you must have them, make them small or otherwise impassable!

Do not make it any easier for heroes, fortune seekers, marshals, military, adventurers, and other rabble to easily undo all that you have labored tirelessly to achieve!

REMEMBER TO LOCK YOUR DOORS![1]

<u>Read this if you value your life</u>:

1. *Have I made myself clear?*[2]
2. *If I have not, prepare to join those fools who have come before you and who have fallen in their pride.*

The Humility of Arrogance

You know that you are great.

I know that you are great.[1]

Move beyond the acceptance of your centrality to the functioning of the macroverse and understand this: if you continue to act upon your arrogance, you will die. Your pride in yourself, your belief in your abilities, and your grave misapprehensions with regard to your capabilities will result in your downfall.

Accept your greatness… fine.

But let this prideful emotion go. Everyone knows it already.

Why else would they let you have dominion over them?

Understand the weakness of your subjects, their frailties, their failings[2], and their desires.[3] Let this humility temper your arrogance and forge your understanding.
Then act accordingly.

At least then you might live.[4]

And your living is what everyone wants, is it not?

Read this if you value your life:

1. *This is of course an assumption, but you were smart enough to read this vaunted tome and that counts for something.*
2. *And there are many.*
3. *I am not, however, saying that you should give your subjects their hearts' desires by any means. After all, this might interfere with your needs.*
4. *And avoid falling prey to some foul scheme intent upon creating your downfall.*

32

On Accepting Advice and Recognizing Terrible Ideas

You don't want to die.

You probably don't wish to be overthrown.

I would guess you would prefer not to be laid low in hand-to-hand combat and then tortured until your will shatters into an unrecognizable fragmented mess.

Nor would you desire flogging, imprisonment, being sent to a penal dimension, crucifixion, having your wealth and power stripped from you, or being made a fool.

You probably don't aspire to being mutilated, cursed, persecuted, tormented, or wearing a dunce cap.

When you were young, you probably didn't dream of growing up to be destitute, needy, worthless, abandoned, or unwanted.[1]

Have a bit of caution.

Villains are not perfect.[2]

We have our faults.[3]

Understand the many urgencies and manifold dangers of your chosen lifework.

They are legion.

You are not.[4]

Don't make your life more difficult than it already is.

Bad advice, just like bad ideas, can spell your end quicker than a sword at your throat, a bullet through your head, or poison in your favorite beverage.

That shimmeringly resplendent power armor battlesuit exquisitely engineered to augment your capabilities by orders of magnitude sounds perfect on paper—until you consider that on the battlefield it will make you a target easily picked out and picked off.[5]

The inordinately complex Rube Goldberg machine you have contrived to eliminate your archrival is a wonder of creative design and innovation—but your time, efforts, and resources could be more effectively spent elsewhere.

The intergalactic governmental seat you so want to see eradicated probably could be destroyed much more effectively without your personal involvement on the ground at the site of its highly defended headquarters... especially without backup.

No matter how wondrous, now matter how promising, now matter how enticing, you must learn to sift the good ideas from the bad, the worthwhile advice from the dregs, the possible from the practical, and the likely from the doomed.

You must also recognize the source of advice given, the potential motivations behind that advice, and whether you will truly benefit from accepting it.[6]

Cultivate clarity in vision, resolution in action, and learn to cut through the crap.

You'll thank me for it.

You'll also live longer.

Read this if you value your life:

1. *Unless of course these are all part of your grand plans. If so, then continue.*
2. *Present company excluded.*
3. *Although they are few.*
4. *This is only an assumption. You may, in fact, be legion.*
5. *And when you realize that your advisors pushing for the technology's adoption may also benefit from your demise.*
6. *Feigning to accept that advice and then entrapping or gaining an advantage over a potential rival is another matter entirely.*

Be Memorable (After All, You Are the Center of the Story)

There are those who say the world has a place for them.[1]

I say, *make a place for yourself.*

You are a *Villain!*[3]
You are the center of the universe.
Everything[4] revolves around you.

Make it happen!
Be unforgettable!
Everyone else struggles through a limited sea of banal sameness and uniformity with no imagination or vision[5], existing on the merest dregs of existence.

Not you!

You soar through the highest realms of self-interest, crushing all competition and obstacles, achieving your heart's desire without compunction or fail!

Do it with style!

Let your legend resound through the cosmos!

Be inimitably inimical!

Whatever you wish to achieve, whatever you hope to accomplish, whoever you wish to rob, whatever you wish to destroy, whatever you want to overthrow, whatever you desire to desecrate, you are capable.
All that is required is a little foresight, not getting in your own way, and letting your enemies stumble before you.[7]

Your mythos awaits.

Read this if you value your life:

1. Probably all warm and fuzzy and full of teddy bears.[2]
2. I despise teddy bears.
3. That capital 'V' was intended.
4. Of importance.
5. I may be contradicting myself here[6] but you get my point.
6. And elsewhere.
7. And then you can trample them underfoot.

Failure is *NOT* the Only Option

First and foremost, there is absolutely nothing wrong with failure, particularly mistakes that you learn from and avoid in the future.[1]

There is a proud legacy of failure in the villainous tradition. In many ways, dizzying mountainous heaps of unending failure *is* the villainous tradition.

I am here to change that.[3]

As nemeses, antiheroes, foils, malefactors, supervillains, and criminals, failure in its many forms, hues, and degrees, holds the advancement and spread of our grand works, our aims and objectives as evildoers, back.[4]

Consider:

Your latest diabolical plan, a magnum opus of sheer terror and villainly villainous villainy, has been thwarted by a motley ragtag band of untrained and untried castoffs including an orphan, a luckless thief, and a prince whose parents perished at your hand decades ago.

Their success has left you spinning in confusion, your well-ordered world of destruction and mayhem tumbling down around you.

Has the time come to plant a garden and dedicate your life to growing rare strains of heirloom seed crops on the verge of extinction?

No!

You recognize those fools' luck for what it was, dumb chance, and get back out there and crush them beneath your hardened heel before they have a chance to wipe the grins off their faces.

Or, take advantage of their guileless ways and overgrown sense of ethical responsibility and entice them into growing that garden for you by impressing upon them the urgency of your horticultural cause while you continue your campaign of destruction.

Whichever path you choose, failure is NOT an option.

Your chaos-inducing economic disruption algorithm has stabilized the markets and brought fiscal and trade stability the world over.

Your oversights and inadvertent improvements in social well-being have left you an outcast in the villainous community.

Do you hang your head in shame and retire to a life of playing competitive video games?

No!

You recognize your failure as an opportunity, reverse engineer your code, and modify and improve upon its functioning such that *you* can capitalize on its workings and corner[7] the markets for yourself.

Your world-spanning empire is in shambles as revolutionaries are overthrowing your regimes at every turn. Even your greatest strongholds of power are folding.

Is it time to give in to the advancing tides of impending progress, egalitarianism, and justice?

No!

Recruit more troops, send out counterrevolutionaries, summon forth denizens from the darkest pits of the Abyss, hire intergalactic mercenaries, bring up your legions of undead, call out your genetically engineered super soldiers from the cryogenic vats, or bring forth the heavy artillery.

Let a rain of destruction usher in a new day!

Or, surprise your foes with flowers in the streets, currency in their pockets, improved infrastructure campaigns, and enhanced social programs.

Either way, failure is NOT an option.

Adventurers are plundering your hordes, sacking your castles, and taking your prized artifacts for their own—stealing your hard(ly)-earned riches away from you.

Do you let your valuables leave your hands and retire to a modest life of ease in the bucolic countryside?

No!

You steal them back!

Send a message that no one takes from you without having worse visited upon them whole orders of magnitude greater than was done to you.

Or, recruit the most successful heroes, and have them reinforce your security systems and fill the various gaps in your defenses.

Regardless, failure is NOT an option.

You have overthrown the crime lord governing a far-reaching illicit organization whose activities range from kidnapping and drug traffic to terrorism, assassination, and black market trade in pre-release videogames.

Do you sit back and rest on your laurels, relishing your accomplishment while the crime boss's old cronies plot your downfall?

No!

You root out those disloyal to you, sending them posthaste to the same unmarked tomb where you interred their boss.

Or, you can win their loyalty along with those of other members of the organization by a combination of successful initiatives, targeted rewards, and the promotion of those who show the greatest promise to provide the most benefit to your own ends.

No matter what, failure is NOT an option!

Failure and its attendant setbacks are the bane to the low and ignoble art of villainy.

As base and demoralizing as failure can be, we cannot let past impediments interfere with future efforts.

While appreciating the failure-laden past, we must ever move to the future...

One where failure is heaped upon our foes.[8]

Read this if you value your life:

1. *It's the ones that can kill you that I am most concerned about.[2]*
2. *That is to say, the ones most likely to happen to a villain.*
3. *You had better be too.*
4. *Plus, we already have bad enough reputations as evildoers without heaping another layer of prejudice onto the pile.[5]*
5. *Being bad is bad enough. Being bad and incompetent is a low we should avoid at all costs.[6]*
6. *Plus, as mentioned above, being incompetent can get you killed.*
7. *And crush.*
8. *Then we will see who is spreading cheer and overflowing with goodness and light.*

Thinking Things Through (and Avoiding Mistakes)

This is your forte, your bread and butter.[1,2]

If you cannot stay one step ahead of your adversaries, then you might as well stop stepping.

Granted, I know there are times when you need to lash out in a rage to destroy all opposition in raging gouts of all-incinerating hellfire.
That's understood.

Sure, there are moments when fits of violence are necessary, and you need to unleash hurricane-force hailstorms of bullets.
This goes without saying.

Obviously, there are instants when you just have to rant, offering a deafeningly explosive tyrannical tirade that leaves your quavering listeners wishing they had been born without the unfortunate faculty of auditory sensation.
This is expected.

But, and this is critical, your impulsivity must be balanced by a lethal dosage of cunning, foresight, and planning.
Sometimes you have to stop a moment, pause, take a deep inhalation, relax, exhale, and think things through.

I know being rational is hard.
I know being ordered is a challenge.
I know being logical incurs quite a bit of stress.
I know strategizing and following through with a set plan can be daunting.

I also know you want to live.

So do yourself a favor.
Slow down.

Make some notes.
Plan ahead.
Be cautious of potential mistakes and counters to your actions.

You'll live longer.

Then you can go back to blowing things up.

I promise.

Read this if you value your life:

1. *Mmm... butter.*
2. *Unless it's not.*

Proper Dress (Why You Don't Need a Costume)

Avoid being a stereotype.[1] Try not to become a caricature of yourself and all you symbolize.[2]

Villains have enough to deal with already.

Just because you're the Grand Galactic Generalissimo, you don't have to always dress in military garb.[5]

Being the Undying Knight of Darkness doesn't mean you must never take off your unholy plate armor.[6]

You may be the Archlich of Eternal Night, but you can still wear something other than tattered robes veiled in a nimbus of gloom.[7]

Though you may be the Blade of Shadow, you don't have to don a full cowl and cloak yourself in an assassin's garb.[8]

Your role as the most feared supervillain in the cosmos does not require you to wear a skintight outfit with arcane sigils on it symbolizing your evilness or power.[9]

Despite leading the most feared cult on the continent, you do not need to dress in your ceremonial High Priest of Doom garb at all times.[10]

And remember, black is not the only color on the spectrum! Have you ever seen a rainbow?

Black isn't even on it!

Branch out! Try something new!

You are a villain!

Set your own trend!

Wear what you want! Wear garb reflective of how you feel!

Be yourself.

Let others follow.

Read this if you value your life:

1. *Let others fall prey to this banality.*
2. *Let this weakness afflict others.*[3]
3. *Then you may use their failings to your advantage.*[4]
4. *Most especially if their downfall is to your benefit.*
5. *Show some originality to the troops!*
6. *If nothing else, think of the smell in there!*
7. *Don't you want to see something other than your own shadows?*
8. *People will know you're a rogue just by looking at you. You don't have to give yourself away.*
9. *Really? How can you even get into that costume—and why would you? How do you expect to intimidate anyone wearing that clown suit?*
10. *How do you eat? All those bones, effigies, and charms have got to get caught in your soup. Unless they provide extra flavor or seasoning?*

Make It Hard for Your Adversaries

You're tired of failure.
I'm tired of failure.
We're *all* tired of failure.

Let's try not to make it so easy for our adversaries.

No matter how vast your resources, no matter how complete your stratagems, no matter how powerful your weaponry, no matter how total your control, no matter how great your force of arms, no matter what depth or degree of influence you have over others, no one villain is in complete control of his[1] actuality.

Despite your earnest efforts, arm-twisting, machinations, predictions, and preparations, things will turn out badly.

Often for you.

Your lackeys will fumble about futilely with even the simplest tasks.
Your investments will sour.
Co-conspirators will develop a conscience.
Random heroes will crash through your door.
Allies will switch sides.
Revolts will challenge your rule.
Rival gangs and various legions will struggle with you for power.
Your fortunes will turn on a whim.
You may even lose your cape.

Take a deep breath.
Take stock of yourself.
Assess your empire.
Reevaluate your underlings.
And try again.

That's all you can do.

Do not *ever* give up.
Do not *ever* give in.
Do not *ever* stop pushing for your goals.

To do so is exactly what your enemies want.

You are in the business of doing exactly what your adversaries *don't* want.

And by doing what your rivals *do not* want you to do, you win.

And make their life as difficult as they would make your own.[2]

Read this if you value your life:

1. *Or her or its.*
2. *Which is an added bonus.*

Don't Be a Victim

How many ways do I have to tell you this?[1]

Why is the most feared individual on the planet[2] always being victimized?

How is the fellest warrior of his generation[3] always failing at the most critical instant when all his many years of planning and training hinge on one moment?

What causes a being that has amassed inordinate amounts of power over generations upon generations to be blind to the obvious: a mistake leading to its ultimate downfall?

Lack of luck?
Lack of fortune?
Lack of vision?
Lack of perception?
Lack of discernment?
Lack of prospects?

Do you want to fail?

No.

The root of most villains' ultimate failure is internal weakness!
And this weakness is the fear of failure itself.

Despite all exterior appearances of power, majesty, intelligence, and foresight, deep down almost all villains want to prove they are better than they actually are—but they are unwilling to make the mistakes required to learn and grow into the true forces of destruction that they are destined to be!

We overreach.
We oversimplify.
We overplan.
We overextend.
We over and over!

Don't feel inferior!
Don't feel like you have something to prove!

So we fail.
So we are occasionally defeated.
So some of our megalomaniacal plans don't work out as we would like.
So some of our treasures are stolen.

Don't be a victim!
Don't start feeling sorry for yourself.
Don't beat yourself up for your own limitations.

Just do what you need to do and the rest will fall into place.

Do you need to cast down a just, kind ruler who has spent a lifetime advocating the needs of the poor and repressed?
Do it!
Don't worry about proving yourself, or about what others may think of you.
Your actions will make that clear enough.
Besides, you will be able to rewrite history after your goals have been achieved.

Do you need to subvert the universal life force in your efforts to transmogrify your material presence into something far greater?
Get it done!
Do not fret about how success or failure will impact the rest of your despotic career.
Your efforts will be judged based on their merits, not your feelings.

Do not give your enemies an opening to bring you down through needless questioning, internal strife, or poor decision-making.
They are already looking for those openings at every opportunity.

Remember, you are the one who victimizes![4]

Read this if you value your life:

1. *Apparently as many as I can get away with until you stop reading and actually go out and succeed in villainy!*
2. *Or any other.*
3. *Or any remembered.*
4. *I hate giving pep talks.*

Pregnable Impregnable Lairs

I don't care how safe or reinforced your fastness is based on your evaluations or those of others.

I don't care how long your keep has withstood the relentless assaults of your enemies.

I don't care how complete the defenses are on your fortress.

Your enemies will always find a way through.[1]

Your best preparation is to have a plan for them when they arrive.

Read this if you value your life:

1. *And let's face it, half of the fun of being a villain is in meeting your rivals face to face.[2]*
2. *And then crushing their dreams.[3]*
3. *Or destroying their souls.[4]*
4. *Or eliminating them outright.[5]*
5. *Or whatever else suits your fancy.*

The Good Guys Don't Always Win

Contrary to popular misconceptions, the good guys don't always win.[1]

This fallacious view is merely the mass delusion of the incompetent, a pitiful wish for reality to be how it is not, a sad consolation for those too weak to seize the chances they are given.

Consider your own record. How does it hold up?

You have conquered whole worlds.
Worlds full of "good guys."
Where are they now? Where are the heroes, the challengers, the blessed kindhearted victors?
Cleaning your boots.
Taking out your trash.
Baking cookies for you.

You have amassed the wealth of nations through guile, trickery, subterfuge, strategy, and ruthless action.
Where are the ethical, the principled, and the just of heart?
Adding to your bottom line.
Helping expand your empire.
Doing whatever they can to hang on and eke out a life under your vast shadow.

"Good guys" may occasionally win… but you *triumph*.

Savor your superiority. Let them wallow in the failures dictated by their own limitations.
You have none.[2]

Read this if you value your life:

50

1. *Although the idea is rather humorous… and can be used to your advantage.*
2. *Worth noting.*

Villains Act, Heroes React

You keep the story moving.

You keep the adventure interesting.

Heroes' lives are great.
Their lives are filled with verdant fields of flowers, butterflies, and rainbows.
Their lives are overflowing with hugging strangers whose hearts are overtopped with generosity, compassion, and love.
Their lives brim with bright-eyed, smiling children frolicking with balloons and bubble gum.

Their lives are boring.

You give meaning to their existence.
You provide them with excitement.
You make their lives worthwhile.
Your efforts cull the weak from the strong and the dull from the bright.
You are the principal motivator for progress and improvement.

Be proud of your accomplishments.
Your actions dictate the tempo of life's unfolding.
Your plans determine the beat and rhythm of the lives of heroes.[1]

Read this if you value your life:

1. *Beat them down![2]*
2. *Or play them as you wish.*

Unleash the Evil!

There are times when you must let the evil flow.

There are instances when you must let overwhelming torrents of evil surge forth from the deepest wellspring of your being.

When unending masses of your enemies rush forward blades bared, an implacable tide seeking to draw you down into the dark, silent depths of the battlefield so that you will never rise again, you must unleash the evil!

When storms of chaos and magic unfettered rage against your fortress, battering your will and shaking your essence, you must unleash the evil!

When enemies plot your downfall at every turn, employing all the vile tricks of honesty, decency, and truth, you must unleash the evil!

BUT...

When you sit down for breakfast, your fork poised over a plate of eggs, toast, and assorted mixed berries, you must NOT unleash the evil!

When you carefully arrange your ledgers, papers, and tomes on your desk, ready to evaluate your various accounts, treasures, and holdings, you must NOT unleash the evil!

When you arrive at your final exam in *Soul Crushing* before graduation from Gormandeus's School for Warlocks and Witchcraft, you must NOT unleash the evil!

When your mother begins recounting the tale of your first foray into evil at your family reunion, a story she has retold hundreds of times before, you MUST NOT unleash the evil![1]

Evil has a time and a place,[2] BUT there are times when evil must be tempered that you may unleash it in the future.[3]

Read this if you value your life:

1. *Okay... maybe you can unleash the evil.*
2. *Namely all the time and every place..*
3. *Refraining from unleashing the evil at all times makes those instances of expression all the more enjoyable.*

Diabolical Plans...

Must never go to waste.

If they did, then how could they be considered diabolical?

Instead, they would be considered mildly irksome.

Not catastrophic.

Or they might be regarded as a complete waste of bad time and evil intent.

That is, only demoralizing to you and your henchmen.

Or they may be viewed as slightly humorous.

Only you won't be laughing.

You must *not* let this happen.

As a bringer of universes of misfortune, one of your principal duties is to never flag, to never fail, and to never underdeliver with your nefarious plans and their realization.

Do your homework before you show up to class.[1] That way you'll be ready when the action starts.

Read this if you value your life:

1. *And by homework I mean preparations. And by class I mean the hurricanes of destruction, galaxies of terror, and soul-crushing defeats that you will be visiting upon your foes.[2]*
2. *Most likely upside their heads [3]*
3. *In the technical parlance.*

Providing a Hero with Something to Do

Heroes are like children. They are always looking for something to do.[1]

Be kind enough to provide them with something to occupy their time, so long as it does not interfere with your true aims and objectives.

They'll feel better.

You will too.[2]

Read this if you value your life:

1. *Options include fell quests, circuitous monster-infested mazes, inimical alien forces brought forth from interdimensional rifts, deadly treasure hunts, halting or defusing any number of potential doomsday devices, preventing assorted catastrophes, rescuing damsels or dudes in distress, averting global shortages in spandex supply, and the like... let your inner evil run wild!*
2. *And this is the fun of being evil... let your creative juices flow![3]*
3. *And your enemies fall!*

Being the Prime Mover

You are the center of your universe.[1]

In fact, the universe revolves around you.

Act like it.

Own your greatness.
Wear the dreadful deadliness of your being like a badge.
Take pride in the majesty of your malefaction.
Extend your baleful presence inexorably outward.

Make the universes of your foes orbit about your gravity, the courses of their actions defined by the universal laws you delineate, and the trajectory of their paths determined by the causes and effects you instill.

Let your adversaries be the puppets and you their master.[4]

You are the cause to your enemies' effect.

Need I say more?[5]

Read this if you value your life:

1. *The universe defined by your being...*[2]
2. *Of course, that you are the center of the multiverse goes without saying.*[3]
3. *Without saying much for logic, rationality, or understanding... but I digress.*
4. *Whatever you do, try not to get tangled up in the strings!*
5. *Because I can.*

Be as Evil as You Can Be

Kicking dogs, taking children's toys, and stealing babies' ice cream…

These are the little things that make villains villainous.

These are the simple pleasures that define our lives.

Really?

Is that the best you can do?

You can do and be more than this.

You can be a true connoisseur of the dastardly.

Plagues, poxes, pandemics, and pustules; rot, infection, and woe; destruction, violence, and villainy; curses, maledictions, and spite; dissembling, embellishment, and propaganda; impropriety, treachery, and corruption… these are the true playthings of the vile.
Exploring any one of which could be a career unto itself.

I suggest employing all these and more.

Frequently.

With utmost skill and precision.

You'll thank me for it.[1]

Read this if you value your life:

1. *But your enemies will not.*[2]
2. *You're welcome.*

Now What?

So, you've caused social collapse on a galactic scale.

You've decimated whole legions of adversaries single-handedly.

Your empire spreads beyond your ability to visit its entirety in your lifetime.

You have amassed more wealth than was present in all the entire generations before your birth.

Your trophy room has grown into a warehouse district spanning several dimensions.

Do you sit on your throne, perched on heaps of gold, gems, treasures, and assorted body parts from fallen heroes, moping, with the lights turned off, because you have nothing to do?

NO!!![1]

The time has come for Plan B.

You do have one or two of those, don't you?[2]

Time to spread your intergalactic empire of fear and terror into a new dimension.

Now may be the prime opportunity to consolidate your power across all crime families.

Perhaps you should consider new markets for your undesirable offerings.

This may be your chance to explore the infernal arcana you have neglected for far too long.

Perchance the lull is the perfect time to push a little capital into evil R&D. There are always bigger, better, and faster ways to unleash mayhem and destruction.

If your own creativity is lacking, take inspiration from the petty fools you regularly crush. Certainly you'll find some worthy insights in the struggles and bickerings of the common.

If not, outsource the evil!
Have fun seeing what torments others can devise for you to achieve.

Who knows, you may find your muse.

Read this if you value your life:

1. *If you cannot, then you might consider changing professions. Otherwise, someone will be gunning for you long before you have a chance to recover.*
2. *You had better have more than one or two backups by this point in your career!*

Think Small

We all love the grand gesture, the consummate expression of our fell vision—*BUT* sometimes what is the most extravagant is not what is most effective.

Although the exultation of watching the blinding incandescence of a megakiloboulder thermonuclear explosion can send chills down your spine, your efforts to overthrow your foes might have been better spent launching fireworks.

Instead, why not consider a targeted strike against the leadership cadre of your rivals?

Then you can launch the nukes to celebrate.

We all love to see our enemies blasted to ash in a hail of laser fire, incinerated by a massive plasma sword, or crushed beneath the treads of gigantic autonomous super robots—but in reality, the resources spent to create these giant homages to your ego could be better spent elsewhere.

If you must have robots, why not small-scale armored humanoid exosuits?

Or, even more efficient, why not self-reproducing nanoswarms?

If done properly, these alternatives can pack a greater punch than the giant robot you so pine after, present a much more elusive target, and allow you to save your hard-earned capital for something much more worthwhile—like your collection of rare orchids, navel lint, torture devices, manacles, hoaxes, or the like.

Everyone would like to have their own personal armada of interstellar cruisers capable of expanding their empire on a multidimensional scale; but imagine all the idiots you would have to tolerate to man those ships, and all the resources required to maintain their health and well-being on extended voyages of conquest.

As villains, we are generally not in the babysitting or social welfare businesses.[1]

Instead, if you have the technology to create interdimensional vessels, why not consider autonomous drones?

In my experience, automatons are much less prone to unhappiness and revolt.

So you would like to cause your most hated adversary's sun to implode, creating a back hole that will tear apart their homeworld, devastate their civilization, and destroy much of their populace.

Who wouldn't?

But wouldn't you also like to make use of your rival's planet and its resources after they're gone?

Why not consider several genetically tailored plagues targeted to eliminate only your foes?

After successful deployment, you'll have a new playground.

Yes, you could crush your enemy to a pulp beneath an impressively hurled massive mountain of raw rock.

But why bother, when a pebble through the eye may be just as effective?

Why waste energy and effort when the only one you're inspiring is yourself?

Just destroy your enemies as effectively as possible and be done with it.

Save the drama for the theater. You have work to get done.

Then you'll have the luxury of all the free time you could want.

And who doesn't like a little extra time?

Read this if you value your life:

1. Your goals may be different from mine, however.

On Henchmen, Underlings, & Minions

What are your goals as a villain?

What are your aspirations as a nemesis?

How can you most destructively and audaciously accomplish your desired ends and endings?

What nefarious schemes are you currently plotting or pondering?

What assets and capital do you need to realize your machinations?

Are you battling with any resource management constraints?

Do you have any hobbies?

Would you like time for some?

All of these concerns and so much more can be addressed with the appropriate utilization of underlings.[1]

Whether you prefer raging hordes, clandestine operatives, special operations units, mercenaries, elite troops, supernatural creatures, undead, automatons, hired help, or cannon fodder, make your life easier[2] with the careful selection of minions.

You will also have the added benefit of sharing the weight of failure among many others.[4]

Success you may claim all for yourself.

Read this if you value your life:

1. *Whether this utilization is voluntary or not, short-term or permanent.*
2. *And so much more fun.*[3]
3. *And, yes, sarcasm is one possible interpretation of this response.*
4. *One of the many perks of leadership.*

Assumptions Can Kill

Good assumptions let you properly frame your strategies for world domination, allow you to quickly assess meddlesome heroes' intentions and possible weaknesses, provide you with the means to quickly sway recalcitrant subjects, overcome particularly irksome obstacles, and much more.

Bad assumptions can get you killed.

You have transubstantiated the corporeal form and now inhabit a nebulous energy state, impervious to physical harm. Fists, blades, arrows, bullets, flames, bombs, and like impediments cannot hurt you.

You assume you are impervious to *all* harm and that your dominion will never end.

Have you ever met a Priest of K'un Lun or an Elven *Aerya'ana*? The things they can do with energy will astound you… and can get you killed.

Your intelligence, cunning, and guile are unmatched. No foe has been able to overcome your wicked stratagems, political maneuvers, or tactical genius.

You assume no one will be able to match your acumen.

Have you ever conversed with a Paratechnological Construct? Entities capable of simulating and modeling the unfolding of the macroverse may be able to match your acuity.

Your feats of arms are legendary. The greatest champions of untold races have fallen at your feet, crushed beneath your heel.

No one can stand before you!

Did you read what I said about Priests of K'un Lun above? If you haven't, maybe you should.

For that matter have you ever tangled with a Dracodaeran *Shaur'Daus*? If not, you really might want to reconsider.

After all, the universe is large, and you do not fill its entirety.

Your arms and armaments are unparalleled. Your exoarmor troops, droid armies, interstellar chaos-class warships, and sentient hunter-killer bots cannot be defeated!

Have you ever seen what a Gnome can do with a bit of elbow grease and a set of pliers? Much less a NUMEN?

Don't get too excited. Your foes may be just as capable as you… if not more so.

Your genetic modifications and mutations have enhanced your capabilities beyond the bounds of mortal ken. You are a god among men!

Your ascendancy will never end!

Calm down. Take a deep breath.

If this happened to you, it can happen to someone else.[1]

Don't let your assumptions be your undoing.

There will always be holes in your logic and understanding.
Find them.
Fill them.
Close them and lock them away in a vault so tight that not even a gold-starved Dwarven locksmith could break in.

Do what you can to survive and thrive despite your limitations.[3]

Read this if you value your life:

1. _And this is the crux of the matter. If something wondrous happened to you that is the source of your power, uniqueness, and survivability, an equivalent or counter can happen to someone else to an even greater degree._[2]
2. _You have been warned._

3. *I know they are few.*[4]
4. *That's why I'm here—to hammer them out in the forge of your greatness.*

Bad Ideas (or How *Not* to Succeed in Villainy)

Let's face it, we all have them.[1]

Some are worse than others.

Some are downright suicidal.

Prepare yourself by knowing which ideas and actions to avoid.

You'll live longer.[4]

What follows are a few bad ideas and common missteps no evil genius, fell overlord, or master strategist should fall prey to on their way to world supremacy, intergalactic domination, or the corner store.[6] Also included are words of warning, mistakes to avoid, and selected offerings of *good* advice.

1. Personally taking revenge or engaging in retaliatory missions. Most especially alone.

   These misguided efforts usually end badly for would-be conquerors.

   If you are at the head of an army, that's one thing. If you butt your head against an army, then the situation is entirely different.

2. Assuming your infallibility.

   Your fallibility is usually demonstrated at the most inopportune moments... at least for you.

3. Imparting a portion of your power into an object or other being—no matter how desirable or enamoring that object or person may be.

Alternately, letting your power leech from you into an object or being.

Both usually end badly for you.

At best, you are weakened. More likely, you have given power to a potential rival or usurper to your throne.

4. Wearing a long cape.[7]

   Especially long capes that are well-nigh indestructible and which can get caught in machinery.

   Not only can your wondrously menacing cape get entangled in metal-toothed, rock-grinders, wood chippers, and disposal chutes, but your adversaries can use it as a handy lever to drag you to the ground.

5. Wearing heavy, cumbersome armor while on water.[8]

   No matter how impressive or intimidating your armor looks.

   Unless you want your vessel to have another potential anchor.

6. Joining or creating a secret society and expecting to keep anything secret… most especially the secret society itself.

7. Limiting your group of most trusted advisors to only those who greatly respect you.

   If someone who despises you can't spot holes in your latest grand scheme, then you may actually have a shot.

8. Not making absolutely certain any slain enemies are honestly and truly dead. I leave it to your discretion on how to establish this with certainty.

9. Flippantly ignoring the advice of your most trusted advisors in moments of crisis.[9]

10. If you must take prisoners, do not place allied groups in one cell or near each other. The last thing you need is for highly trained, like-minded individuals to escape and unleash revenge from inside your inner sanctum.

11. Playing nice… or fair.

   That's what heroes do.

   You are not a hero.

12. Trusting what your enemies tell you—no matter how flattering it may be, or how much you want to believe what they say.

   You lie to them all the time. Why wouldn't they return the favor?

13. Understimating what a determined individual can do.

   After all, you are a determined individual and you have conquered worlds, overthrown dynasties, and discovered how to prevent cereal from getting soggy in milk.

14. Failing to ensure your minions know how to accurately fire their guns, bows, crossbows, slingshots, boomerangs, or whatever implement of destruction you have bestowed upon them.

   Remember, good guys seldom miss.

   This is a fundamental law of the universe.

15. Leaving the cogs, gears, wheels, pulleys, moving parts, and other mechanisms in your latest doomsday device open and uncovered. For reasons that should be obvious, this may not be in your best long-term interests. This applies equally to chemical vats, poisonous urns, pits of toxic sludge, and the like.

Remember, safety first![10]

16. Broadcasting your vulnerabilities, weaknesses, and limitations. These matters are not ones you want to be honest about.

    Thankfully, you're a villain.

    Lying about your frailties, on the other hand, is always a good idea. Seeing the look on your adversary's face when he thinks he has you and then realizes he's wrong is priceless!

17. Allowing outside employees, hirelings, or contractors into your inner sanctum.

    All maintenance, security details, and renovations for your lair should be performed by permanent internal staff. Any purported replacements, supplemental help, or assistants should immediately pass a security check or be granted permanent resident status: interred underground.

18. Completely neglecting your populace.[11] Social neglect leads to willing allies for your enemies. As much as it may pain you to do so, repair those slums, ghettos, blighted regions, and tenements—that way your enemies will not have conveniently located areas of your cities in which to hide, recruit allies, and mount hostile activities.

    If you must neglect someone, neglect everyone. That way at least the truth will be readily apparent to all: that everyone is your enemy and will be treated as such.

19. Deploying your latest doomsday device in a fit of rage before you've checked to make absolutely certain that it is fully functional.

    The last thing you need is your world-annihilating blaster ray blowing up in your face.

Also, backup power supplies are your friend.

20. Forgetting your body armor.

    Ever!

    You never know when one of your allies, consorts, friends, or enemies will try to stab you in the back.

21. Falling for the same trick twice.

    Take notes if you have to, or write a journal and study it every night.

    Villains look bad enough already without acting like bumbling simpletons.

22. Relying on a single means of escape.

    Do this under no conditions!

    Not ever!

    Using decoys to confound your chosen means of escape is even better.

23. Accepting a challenge from your enemy.

    Accepting a challenge from a hero is something you do *after* you've killed them.

24. Relying on allies.

    They will always let you down.

    Having a conscience kills... you.

    Allies are no different.

25. Leaving your plans for world domination lying around where even the untrained cleaning staff could conveniently intercept your ideas.

    If you must have copies of your master plans lying around, give them uninteresting labels like "shoe polish recipe," "paint choices," or "veterinary records."

    Place your most nefarious project labels on folders for documents like tax records, receipts, and favorite recipes.

    With this ruse, after any infiltration, you'll be able to follow the trail of pulled-out hair to your despondent enemy crying in the corner beneath a pile of meaningless papers.

26. Worrying about capturing enemies alive.

    This is not a matter to concern yourself with.

    Period.

27. Ignoring an important message or messenger.

    You can do that after you've heard what they have to say.

28. Forgoing all strategy, logic, and decision-making capabilities while under pressure.

    That's what you do the rest of the time.

The macroverse is filled with bad ideas. You need only examine the history of villainy to discover most of them.[12]

You have been warned.

Read this if you value your life:

1. *Yes, even you. No one is criticizing you here.*[2]
2. *Well, we're not criticizing you and laughing about it.*[3]

3. *At least not directly to your face.*
4. *As a villain, despite popular convention, your job is NOT to discover every bad idea under the sun. That is the job of Paratechnologists.*[5]
5. *There are more bad ideas to be discovered under the sun than there are suns. Paratechnologists are hard at work uncovering both... suns and bad ideas.*
6. *This is by no means a complete list. I am sure that your creative incompetence will discover untold worlds of other means to fail.*
7. *Unless you have a quick-release clasp.*
8. *Unless you don't need to breathe, your armor includes technological accommodations for alternate environments, or your armor can come off quickly.*
9. *This is what you do when there is, in fact, no crisis.*
10. *Second, and third.*
11. *Just the thought of being nice hurts me. Make it stop!*
12. *See, for example,* The Book of Bad Ideas – A Villain's Guide to Anti-Idiocy *by Audentatious Ludicraneum.*

Planning for Success (While Accepting Failure)

Heroes save the day.

Villains ruin it.

In order to actually ruin the day, living to see the day's end really helps.[1]

The obstacles you face and overcome will define you.[2]

Being defined will give you the confidence to wear that new skintight unibody evil overlord costume you've been pining after for the past decade.

Then, not only will you feel successful, you will be motivated for further successes.

Where is there room for failure amidst all that success?[4]

And, really, you don't have to be defined to be definitive.

You just want to be the ultimate evil you can be.[8]

Read this if you value your life:

1. *And allows you to ruin a few more for your adversaries.*
2. *Facing and overcoming adversaries also makes you feel better.*[3]
3. *And potentially deepens your treasury, increases your power base, eliminates competitors, improves your stature, broadens your opportunities, and gives you a bit more free time to bask in the glow of evil.*
4. *What, in the name of all that is unholy, am I talking about?*[5]
5. *I really have no idea... have I been zapped by an anticogitation ray gun?*[6]

6. *A dunce bomb? A confusion cloud? A swarm of synapse-disabling nanobots? Is there a Paratechnologist phasing in and out of existence nearby, inflicting his own misguided delusions upon my mind-state?[7]*

7. *Let me restate. Having confidence in yourself, whether you succeed or fail, will allow you to press forward and ultimately persevere despite the raging avalanches of unending failure that bury most villains' short-lived, uninspired careers.*

8. *"Be the ultimate evil you can be" is copyright Saedeus Moerdencanum. Payments for licensing rights and usage can be sent to my shell bank account per linked instructions.*

In the Company of Villains

Do what you must to advance your interests.[1]

Villains are taciturn, duplicitous, manipulative, dangerous, greedy, deceitful, lecherous, parsimonious, and treacherous. And that's on the best of days.

Don't give away too much, for your cohorts will gladly take what you offer.[2]

Don't let them.

Make certain every situation works to your advantage.

Ultimately, if that means being by yourself, then so be it.

That you are better company than anyone else goes without saying.

Read this if you value your life:

1. *Luckily, this is no different than your normal behavior.*
2. *And more.*

Horrible Haircuts

Aren't things hard enough already without you choosing an awful, ill-advised coiffure or hair sculpt?

I know the combination of a buzz cut with spiked hair on top—accentuating the shoulder-length mullet in the back—looked great in the hairstyle selection catalog, but is it a good idea?
Especially with your lanky, rank, unwashed hair?
Sure, you don't even need styling gel to spike your hair considering all the grease, but do you even want to try?

Do you really want to make things even more difficult for yourself?

Look at yourself in the mirror.[1]

You are evil.

Chances are, you're not particularly attractive.[2]

Women and children run from your presence.

Flowers wilt when you near.

Foggy plumes shadow your every step.[3]

Think of how easy your poor hygiene and fashion choices will make it for torch-wielding mobs carrying random farm implements to taunt you as they ineffectually try to storm your castle.

Then again, maybe horrible haircuts aren't so bad.

Your image can't get much worse.[4]

Who am I to judge?

Read this if you value your life:

78

1. *Assuming it doesn't break.*
2. *Okay, maybe you are, but it's enjoyable to have fun at another person's expense.*
3. *And I'm not talking about your smell.*
4. *Maybe that works for you. Go with it!*

Know Your Opposition

I'm not asking you to invite your rivals to dinner.
Nor am I asking you to befriend your enemies.

These things are beneath you. Unless, of course, doing depraved acts of kindness and generosity are part of your diabolical plans. Then mingle and schmooze away.

I am asking you to do the background work that will allow you to crush your opposition.
Then you won't have to deal with them anymore.

Unfortunately, enemies are like seasons: they just keep coming back whether you want them to or not.[1]

Read this if you value your life:

1. *By constantly culling your foes, you can keep them weak, manageable, and under control.*[2]
2. *Then everyone that matters wins.*[3]
3. *This means you.*

Idiot Proofing Your Lair

I am assuming you are not an idiot.[1]
You will, however, be working with them.

For your sake[2], I suggest keeping your minions and underlings alive as long as possible.[3]

This process may take some consideration and investment on your part. Consider your minions, their foibles, and weaknesses in your fortress design:

Do you work with zombies?
Avoid open pits, magma flows, crevasses, high bridges, open caldera, mountain peaks, and the like.
Flat open areas are your principal design vehicle.

Are your underlings humanoids of less than average intelligence?
Avoid convoluted mazes, complicated devices and interfaces, and other sources of confusion and conflict.
Treat your design layouts as with zombies above.

Do you ride a dragon?
Depending on the type, you will need an area almost on the opposite end of the spectrum from that favored by zombies—one with room to spread wings and fly, mountainous regions, areas to perch, and access to food, lots of food.
Peaks near great plains are excellent for maintaining the diet of your dragons, as are steady streams of adventurers.

Do you employ sophisticated machinery, robots, equipment and the like?
Avoid harsh exotic environments[5] that may degrade or otherwise interfere with the performance of your devices.
While the highly corrosive acidic planet orbiting a nearby sun may be unsuitable for your needs, perhaps the derelict moon next door may be more amenable to your plans of galactic conquest.

These are but a few of many examples. As difficult as it may be to think of others, tailor the design of your fastness not only to your needs but to the needs of those unfortunate enough to work for you.

Then everyone will be happy (or as close to such an irksome feeling as you allow)… most especially you.[6]

Read this if you value your life:

1. *This may be a stretch.*
2. *Not so much theirs.*
3. *As uninteresting, unappealing, and irksome as associates may be, they are generally required to succeed in your endeavors.[4]*
4. *Feel free to get rid of them when their use has expired.*
5. *No matter how alluring, intimidating, or otherwise attractive such a place may be to your highly refined sense of decorum and taste.*
6. *Because, in the end, that's all that really matters anyway.*

Avoiding Delusion (Especially Your Own!)

As much as this admission pains me to admit, villains are as prone to delusion as the most common[1] of sentient beings.

In fact, we may be more so.[2]

That we have the imagination to deceive ourselves is to our credit.

That we often die of unrealistic expectations, overconfidence, and poor decisions is not.

Recognition of this potential weakness can be the source of your greatest strength.[3]

In fairness to villains, because the sweep of our vision tends to include a grander conception than that of those less adventurous and forward-thinking, the dizzying acmes of our perspectives are bound to be a bit more treacherous than those of the pedestrian unenlightened— hence we have a slightly heightened proclivity toward misapprehension and somewhat delusional thought.

As grandly world-shaking as your conceptions may be, as all-encompassing and staggeringly momentous as your plots and schemes are, as epoch-shattering as your aspirations will be, your efforts must be balanced by practicality and sound judgment.[4]

Before you decide to change the world, consider all the ways you will fail trying.

This difficult soul-searching[6] may save you a bit of time and frustration before you invest too heavily in the many ways you can flounder, blunder, and meet with disaster.

More importantly, improving your decision-making process may make those grand visions a bit more likely.

The world trembles with anticipation.

Read this if you value your life:

1. *And uncommon.*
2. *Sometimes the truth hurts… badly.*
3. *And you should always be looking to increase your strength!*
4. *If you can't do this appraisal yourself, I suggest an intern. They work for peanuts (or coffee), will do almost anything you ask, and offer a naïvely innocent perspective on all things evil that is counterbalanced by a shrewdly ruthless appreciation of practicalities. Also, they are good at disappearing when you don't want them around.*[5]
5. *I can think of many institutions of higher learning that would gladly farm out their best and brightest to your evil intern program for but nominal considerations.*
6. *Actually having a soul is optional.*

Swords and Cudgels May Break My Bones but Diatribes Will Never Hurt My Ego

As a villain, you are above the merest prattlings of your adversaries, the recriminations of would-be heroes, and the admonishments of aspiring Samaritans.

Accept these words as the dross they are.

Do not let the barbs and clever ploys of your foes force your hand.
Crush them like the insects they are.[1]

Do not let their foibles sully your character.
Your conscience is dirty enough already.[2]

Do not let their heartfelt, if misguided, pleas sway you.
You have more important matters to consider.

Do not let their ruses and arguments divert you from your intended course.
You have goals to achieve and these miscreants are in your way.
Move them.

And this is the truth of the matter. If your oppositions' accusations and ruminations mattered, you would have considered them.

But they don't matter and you do.

Move on.

There's evil to be done.

Read this if you value your life:

1. *Then, when you are done and have moved on to other more important matters, you may gladly wash your hands of the matter entirely.*
2. *Or spotlessly clean depending on your view.*

Why No One Matters But You

As a villain, you live for one purpose: your own. [1]

Nothing else matters.

Certainly, there are potentially consequential considerations like food, water, shelter, sleep, air, and finding a way to provide those things in perpetuity, but even those things are of minor concern compared to your overriding need—the need to shape the universe to your ends.

If you choose to put your faith, your belief, in others, you will live a life of disappointment. If you are extremely fortunate, others' needs may align with your own and you may realize your dreams of destruction and dismay.
Odds are, this misguided hope of a fortuitous alignment of chance and your desires will not happen. At best, this looming disappointment will only further fuel your fires of discontent.

Avoid potential heartache and pain.
Believe in yourself, and put your efforts into your own accomplishments. Then, at worst, the only one you will blame for any failures will be you. More likely, you will continue to improve and move ahead toward your nefarious goals, one painfully agonizing effort at a time.
In the end, the rewards you reap will be your own, and the glory you achieve yours alone to share.

I never was good at sharing.

Chances are, you aren't either.

Read this if you value your life:

1. _Do not allow yourself to waver or be distracted from your intent no matter how shiny the object proffered._

87

Last Words

Life is full of conflicts.

As a villain, you will be in more confrontations than most.

The more aggressive your vision, the higher the likelihood of clashes.

Be prepared for this truth.

Your success is bound to your reputation. When facing your adversaries, choose your words wisely.

For instance, *"I'll get you!"*, although an effective sentiment, just doesn't have the same force or result as *"I will tear your soul apart!"*

Choose your words carefully. They are often how you will be remembered.

Give your enemies judiciously chosen barbs, and reap the rewards of watching the import of your declamations unfold on their unprepared visages.

Your words, especially words before and after confrontations, should be powerful enough to break through your foes' mindsets, cut through delusion, and bring the light of understanding to their limited views.

Make of your words an opportunity to change your enemies to your benefit.
Use your words to create an advantage for yourself.

Properly chosen last words can be one vehicle to the future you wish to create.[1]

Read this if you value your life:

1. *Also, well-chosen cheap shots, insults, and rejoinders are fun to deliver.*[2]
2. *Which, in turn, gives you more incentive to deliver them.*[3]
3. *Which gives you greater motivation to meet with conflict and ultimately further your reputation and aims.*

Last Last Words

You are going to die.[1]

As a villain, you are probably going to die sooner than most.

In fact, the grander your vision, the greater the risks.

Be prepared for this fact.

As an evildoer, people bend over backward to listen to your words. The populace wants to hear you!

Make sure your last words are memorable. Let your last words live in infamy… the perfect reflection of your life, your views, and your aims.

Whole societies can turn on a word.

Read this if you value your life:

1. *If this is a revelation to you, you need to reconsider your career choice.[2]*
2. *Quickly.*

A Word on Final Battles & Confrontations

Just kill the guy (or gal) already!

No talking!
No life story!
No detailed exposition on the difficulties your soon-to-be erstwhile opponent has introduced to your plans, objectives, aims, endeavors, yada-yada ad infinitum!

Take him out with utmost expedience while he, she, or it is most vulnerable![1]

What are you doing standing around?
Finish him already!
Can I be any more clear?

Gloat when your enemy is dead and only when you are absolutely certain of it!

Read this if you value your life:

1. *Now!*

Happily Never After

Happiness is a measure of stagnation, an appreciation and acceptance of the status quo.

If you were entirely happy with things as they are, then from where would your motivation for domination derive?

If you were content with your sorry lot in life, where would your drive to exceed, surpass, endure, and prosper originate?

If you were pleased with idyllic indolence, where would your relentless desire to manifest and realize your will stem?

Happiness, and the accepting torpor it represents, runs counter to the intrinsic order and expression of the multiverse.
Life, events, and the universe move ever forward.
So do you.[1]

Evil is a drive onward.
Happiness is an end.

May your implacable motivation and evilness never end.

May you never be happy.

Read this if you value your life:

1. *You are an agent of entropy. Embrace your destiny.*[2]
2. *The more successful organisms and species are those that contribute the greatest to increasing universal entropy.*[3]
3. *Welcome to the rolls of the most prosperous.*

92

Glossary of Terms

People, Places, and Things

Abyss – a general name often used for extradimensional regions home to daemonic creatures of Darkness and despair. Also called *nether realms*.

Adamantium – an exceedingly strong magical metal.

Aerie – a name commonly used for the peaks and summits claimed by dragons as their homes.

Aeromancy – the study of the air and its currents, the manipulation of its energies, and the fashioning of airships.

Aerya – literally, "Light" or "air." An Elven term for the living energy of the universe. The concept of *Aerya* encompasses all forms of magical energetic expression in a single totality from the universal source to the personal creation—both chi and Yuan-chi. See also *Yuan-chi* and *chi*.

Aerya Etherum – literally, "highest air" or "highest breath." Alternatively, "first breath" or "source of breath." An Elven term for the source of the *Aerya*: the formless, boundless Void, source of limitless potential. See also *Wuji*.

Age – any extensive period of time. Typically thought of as representing one thousand years, though events of particular significance may also define its limits.

Airship – magically powered ships in as many shapes as the mind can imagine found plying the air currents and trade routes throughout Ea'ae and beyond. See also *aeromancy*.

Alchemical – Paratechnological study revolving around understanding the higher chemistries of the macroverse's functioning. Just as physical laws govern natural phenomena, and metamagical laws govern magical occurrences, alchemical laws govern the interactions between the two.

Allomorph – a being capable of taking on various shapes and guises, potentially augmenting its own intrinsic abilities, while retaining its primary core awareness, sense of self, and intelligence. The *Jira S'al Alann* are one such example.

Antientropics – the study of creating energy and adding energy back to systems, devices, and entities.

Anubaraëthi – literally, "Spawn of the Shadow," or "Shadow made manifest." A general Elven name for greater, sentient daemons. Sometimes called *Dread Lords*.

Anubavaeri – literally, "Spawn of the Flame," or "Spawn of the Fire." An Elven name for powerful daemons of flame.

Anuvaerya – literally, "Children of the Light." An Elven name for those Elves who have willingly left the bounds of the body to explore the realms of the mind and spirit. The existence of *Anuvaerya* is a closely guarded secret, known only to a few Elf-friends outside the Elven people.

Anuvatali – literally, "Children of the Dawn," or "Children of the New Morn." An Elven name for the half-Elven children of Men and Elves born on Ea'ae.

Anuvatari – literally, "Children of the Sun." An Elven name for those Elves who first came to Ea'ae.

Anuvatari'aliana– literally, "of one voice with the Children of the Sun" or "friend-kin of the Children of the Sun." An Elven name for those people of any race taken in by the Elves and taught something of their ways, or those who are trusted and respected as Elf-kin.

Archfiend – a general name for a daemon, particularly in reference to powerful daemons that have usurped dominion over lesser representatives of their own kind.

Archlich – a particularly powerful lich, often a powerful deceased practitioner of magic. See *lich*.

Archmage – a highly accomplished or powerful magician.

Archmathematics – higher order mathematics, modeling, and cognitive frameworks used in Paratechnological studies.

ARMED – Allomorphic Recombinatorial Multidimensional Extravehicular Drones. A flexible, multi-faceted, shape-changing drone system invented by Spreesprocket. Also called *sentry drones*.

Art – a calling, particularly one magical in nature.

Baera – "Brendle the All-Father" in the tongue of the Dwarves.

Baera'Dur – literally, "Brendle's bulwark" in the tongue of the Dwarves. Called *Dreadnaughts* by Men.

Baeradun – a legendary Dwarven hero known to burst into flames. Sometimes called "Burning Beard".

Beyond – a general term for other dimensions in the multiverse, often in reference to the nether realms. See *Abyss*.

Biomimetics – an area of Paratechnological research focusing on the understanding of biological functions, their governing principles, improvement, and alteration.

Blade Master – a highly proficient teacher of hand-to-hand combat in the Home Guard.

Blade Singer – see *Caer'collas*.

Bor'Banna – literally, "bearded demon." A name for the Dwarven masters of the axe, imbued by the remnants of power from Brendle's fire.

Bot – short for robot, particularly with regard to Paratechnological clockwork devices made by Tinkerers that may or may not manifest synthetic intelligence capable of independent thought.

Brendle – The All-Father. Dwarven god of the forge and, in the eyes of the Dwarves, the creator of the known universe. Called *Baera* in the tongue of the Dwarves.

Brendle's Flame – see *Brendle's Spark*.

Brendle's Spark – the remaining embers from Brendle's original flame and forge when Brendle first wrought the universe under hammer, anvil, and flame. The remaining embers even now bring forth life and magic into the universe. Also, the fires at the heart of the *Daerdaana'Duin*, the *Bor'Banna*'s highest known skill, where the exponent merges directly with Brendle's flames. Also called *Brendle's Flame*. An analogue to *Aerya* and Yuan-chi in Dwarven cosmology.

Brendle's Tears – the finest of Dwarven ales. Reputed to be so wondrous and flavorful that Brendle himself cries tears of joy and amazement with each sip.

The Cabal –A sinister alliance of dark mages, fallen Priests, extradimensional beings, and other creatures of might bent on not only domination but power. Known by many other names, including the Order of the Lidded Eye, the Fallen, the Light Fallen, the Order of the Burning Eye, and the Order of the Hooded Gaze. Called Liúxīng Làngrén by the Priests of K'un Lun. Often symbolized by a blazing sigil of a closed eye.

Caer'collas – a Q'sharian blade master. Often called *Blade Singers* by those who watch their masterful interplay of magic and blade work.

Champion of Light – a general honorific for those who have earned great esteem fighting the forces of Darkness. Also, a title for one of great accomplishment within the Dalaren Ka.

Chi – Qi; breath, air, or vapor of particular significance in Taoism and Eastern medicine. From a Taoist perspective, the chi is the vital energy or life force that enlivens and pervades all things. Chi gung—chi kung or qigong—are exercises to build and strengthen chi flow. Along with shen and ching, one of the Three Treasures essential to human life. Chi is a less subtle and refined form of the Yuan-chi, the universal potential. The fire that does not burn.

Clockwork – a general name for a particular branch or type of Paratechnology focusing on magically animated contraptions of any shape, size, and function, often resembling machines and robots but not limited to any specific shape. A particular specialty of Gnomish Paratechnological Tinkerers.

Common – see *Common Tongue*.

Common Tongue – a universal language used across Ea'ae to facilitate nonmagical communication. Also called *Common*.

Craft – higher magical skills. An umbrella term inclusive of various branches of magic including unique talents and abilities native to particular races, guilds, and tribes.

DADD – Dwarves Against Drunk Dragons. Also, Dragons Against Drunk Dwarves.

Daemon – a general name for extradimensional creatures with hostile intent or for those otherworldly creatures that feed and prey upon the energies of the living. Also called *infernals*.

Daerdaana'Duin – literally, "to become the heart of fire" or "to become the heart of the forge". One of the highest skills of the *Bor'Banna*, wherein the practitioner wreaths himself in the flames of Brendle's forge, becoming a direct manifestation of Brendle's power and one with its heat, energy, and vitality. In times of old, these warriors cloaked themselves in flames, striking down foes directly with Brendle's might. See *Brendle's Spark*.

Daer'Duin – literally, 'heart of fire' or 'heart of the forge'. Given Dwarven name for Slate Flintforge.

Dagron Grey Beard – a famous Dwarven *Dur'kazak* of old.

Darkness – a general term for those beings opposed to the Light and Life it engenders and who would subvert, pervert, or otherwise mar Its presence and manifestation. Also a general term for the corruption of the energy of life, the Light, itself.

Delving – a general name for any Dwarven city or outpost. See also *undermount*.

Deur Spricken Sprack – Gnomish for "the Omnispark." See also *Phlogiston* and *Omnispark*.

Djazoth Al'Zann – a world conquering antihero, cultivator of rare orchids, and collector of stuffed bunnies.

Doerdaana'Duin – literally, "the dance of the heart of fire" or "to dance in the heart of the forge". One form of Dwarven axe work known for its fluid strikes and counters, commonly used by particularly adept *Bor'Banna*.

Dragonflight – a group of dragons living and moving together.

Dragons – along with the *Aeryn D'al*, one of the oldest races of Ea'ae. Steeped in magic and power, dragons are feared by all who cross their path. As complex as they are storied, dragons are as diverse as their characters and can wield power rivaled only by the gods themselves.

Drake – dragon.

Dread Lord – a general name for higher-order, more powerful daemons granted intelligence and power far beyond their peers. Called *Anubaraëthi*, Children of the Shadow, by Elves.

Dreadnaught – a Dwarven warrior specializing in heavy combat. Utilizing enchanted, rune-etched full plate armor along with two-handed axes, hammers, and maces, Dreadnaughts earn their place at the fore of the battlefield by fighting against the most implacable foes. Famous as much for their rallying battle cries and songs—along with their fear-inducing chants and dirges—as for their blades. Called *Baera'Dur* in the tongue of Dwarves.

Drothman – a famous Dwarven hero.

Druids – protectors of the wilds, guardians of nature, and lovers of freedom. First students of the *Indural*.

Dunédâne – literally, "deep delver". Name for the Dwarves among their own kind and the Karadüm.

Duraeleon – "The Light Bringer", bane of Adrael the Black, ancient axe of Ithilieon. Wielded by Slate Flintforge.

Durden – literally, "valiant heart". A Dwarven rune that serves to protect against fear and indecision when properly enchanted.

Durin – a famous Dwarven hero from times of yore.

Dur'kazak – literally, "fire shaper." A Dwarven master smith skilled in the art and craft of metallurgy, elemental magics, and rune crafting known as *Karaduen*.

Dwarves – along with Elves, Gnomes, and Men, one of the four most prominent races on Ea'ae. Dwarves are short, hearty, and solidly built, and are known for their ability to work metal. They excel at reading the earth and mining. Their keen knowledge of metals and runes allows for the creation of powerful works of Craft. Also called *Dunédâne*.

Ea'ae – "The world." Home to magical creatures and races of many shapes, cultures, and forms. Also, an exceptional book series.

EGAD – see the *Every Gnome's Anti-Intelligence Device*.

Elf-kin – Those people of any race taken in by the Elves and taught something of their ways. Sometimes called Elf-friends or *Anuvatari'aliana* in the tongue of the Elves.

Elves – a fey race at home among the trees and dells of Ea'ae. Elves are a race of great Craft and knowledge that made peace with the land long before the coming of Men and Dwarves and many other sentient races.

It is said that magic is the lifeblood of the Elves. Often called Lords of the Wood or Tree Singers by Men, although not all Elves are indeed *Iyela*. Those Elves on Ea'ae are the *Anuvatari*.

The Enemy – Ur'Daus, the Darkness between dimensions. Also known as the Creeping Shadow, Destroyer of Light, the Umbral Lord, the Devourer of Worlds, among many other names and curses.

ENNIS – see *Epistemic Noetic Numenetic Integrating Summator*.

Epistemic Noetic Numenetic Integrating Summator – a multifunctional Gnomish device with capabilities ranging from measurement and systematic evaluation of phenomena, data analysis, computation, and communication to independent reasoning, learning aid, thought transference, and toothbrush. Also called *ENNIS* for short.

Every Gnome's Anti-Intelligence Device – a Paratechnological defensive system, suitable for espionage, surveillance, and camouflage, added to items ranging in size from personal armor to airships. The Every Gnome's Anti-Intelligence Device replicates the surrounding environmental variables and superimposes them over the object protected by the defensive system, rendering it indistinguishable from its surroundings. Sometimes referred to as EGAD or, more specifically and to add to the general air of confusion and embellishment around Gnomish devices, as the Every Gnome's Anti-Intelligence Clandestine Apparatus version 3.1, Corvette Class.

Evility – the expression of the primacy of an individual's needs and interests before the needs and interests of the group or placing the needs of one society ahead of another. The opposite of civility.

Extrabiology – the extension and expansion of biological systems, processes, and representations.

Face of the Mountain – a Dwarven term for an unreadable, stoic visage, as unchanging and unyielding as the mountain rock, particularly suited for floundering and confounding others.

Festival of the Clans – a large gathering of Dwarven clans filled with celebrations, competitions, reunions, feasting, drinking, sharing of lore, addressing of grievances, and forging of alliances.

Fiersayne – the brood and broodmates of Cersaegian.

Flashwhistle Boomblaster – A Gnomish Paratechnologist known for his particularly explosive zest for discovery and knack with incendiary devices.

Fria al'Othra – literally, "eyes of true vision." An Elven term for the universal perspective of the *Iyela*.

Früea – a Dwarven master artisan. The skills of a *Früea* range from creating fine jewelry and ornamentation to complex magical and mechanical artifices.

FTP – faster than physics. Gnomish Paratechnological communications system that allows communications faster than allowed by the (Non)Standard Model of physics.

Future history – the Paratechnological study of outcomes and possibilities.

GastroGnome – Gnomish lover of fine foods.

Gnomes – a race of short stature but of broad mind known for their creativity, imagination, and Paratechnological aptitude. Originators of Paratechnology, famed Tinkerers, often unable to leave well enough alone. Distant relatives of Dwarves.

Gnomeproof – a Dwarven colloquialism for foolproof.

Gnomosphere – Gnomish term for the noosphere.

GPE – Gnomish Protective Equipment.

Günda – literally, "Dwarf excrement." An Orcish curse.

Henosis – a theurgical practice whose ultimate aim is unification with and expression of the Divine Light.

Homeworld – planet of origin or primary habitation for a race, species, or group.

Hröthe – literally, "divine healing". A Dwarven *Karaduen* offering a one-time boon of healing from a grievous or debilitating wound.

Human – see *humanity*. A general name for an individual member of any of the sentient races on Ea'ae.

Humanity – a general name for all humanoid races on Ea'ae. Men, Dwarves, Gnomes, *Indural,* and other sentient races of Ea'ae are included under this broad description. As a naturalized race, Elves, too, are considered part of Humanity, although they are genetically distinct from the other humanoid races.

Hürn – literally, "evil's bane". A Dwarven rune used for protection from evil.

Idealized engineering – the practical translation of Paratechnological ideas to actuality.

Illdrassil – literally, "Spire of the Heavens" or "Tree of Heaven" in the Old Tongue of Men. The home of the Council, Tellanon's ruling body and the Home Guard. A vast repository of magical energies that empowers the city in the sky.

Indural – one trained in the magic, lore, and woodcraft of the forest giants.

Infernal – a daemon.

Iyela – an Elven lorekeeper, wonder worker, tree singer, and shaper. Known for their ability to commune with the spirit of trees and request the boon of their heartwood, the *Aeryn Sh'al*. Called Tree Singers by Men.

Jira S'al Alann – literally, "People of the Imagining". A race of changelings able to shift their guise and abilities depending upon their magical development and attunement. See also *allomorph*.

Karaduen – a Dwarven word meaning "Light's ward" or "Light's seal." Special Dwarven runes and symbols often employed by *Dur'Kazak* and *Kor'Dannan* in the crafting of artifacts and the creation of spells and enchantments.

Kazzak – literally, "marks of honor" in the tongue of the Dwarves. Symbols, tokens, and items of repute woven into a *Bor'Banna*'s beard as badges of honor and accomplishment. Also common among other Dwarves.

Khuerkanna – a famous Dwarven general known for his triumphant last stand against the Orcs and their allies in the Battle of the Broken Blade.

Kiloboulder – a Gnomish unit of force, energy output, and weight.

Koerdian Cave Bear – a species of gigantic cave bear particularly respected by Dwarves for their strength, perseverance, and indomitable spirit.

Kor'Dannan – Dwarven Priests of Brendle given the keeping and wisdom of his fires, Brendle's Spark. Fierce warriors equally adept at healing and providing succor.

Lich – undead beings sustained by twisted magical energies.

Life – all living beings taken as a whole.

The Light – the ambient energy of the universe; the energy of Life enlivening all of existence. Considered holy, sacred, and heavenly. See also *Aerya*, *chi*, ching, dalare, *Deur Spricken Sprack*, *Omnispark*, *Phlogiston*, shen, *Brendle's Spark*, and *Yuan-chi*.

Loess – literally, "Heaven's shielding". A protective Dwarven rune meant for use against supernatural forces.

Ludaceous Vaer Mordicanum – wondrous scribe, scholar, and luminary. One of the greatest intellects of his or any generation.[1]

Mulogo's note:

1. *Or so he thinks.*

Luerdan – literally, "troll dung" in the tongue of the Dwarves.

Macrocosmos – see *macroverse*.

Macroverse – the totality of multi-dimensional existence, inclusive of all planes, alternate universes, and extradimensional regions. See *multiverse*. Also megacosm or macrocosmos.

Magic – the translation of the possible into the actual, the imagined into the real. The three primary components of magical practice are often understood as: *belief,* faith that an individual can take an active part in universal creation; *intent* (or will), the shaping of this belief to guide in creation; and *imagination*, the vision or desired outcome made possible by belief and shaped by intent.

The wellspring of magic is universal energy. Depending upon the tradition, this source is known as Yuan-chi, Brendle's Spark, Phlogiston and the Omnispark, *Aerya*, and Light, among others. This universal energy is often understood as the source and fuel of life, the chi. Sometimes broken into greater and lesser magics referencing the differentiation between the universal source energy—Yuan-chi, Phlogiston, *Aerya*, Light, and celestial or divine magics—and the intrinsic ambient energies of life: the chi.

See also *Yuan-chi, chi, Brendle's Spark, Phlogiston* and *Omnispark, Aerya*, and *the Light*.

Major and Minor Shielding – a complex combination of spells serving to protect the recipient from arcane damage and hostile spells (the Major Shield); while also guarding against physical damage, impacts, blows, cuts, and the like (the Minor Shield).

Mauguer – a Dwarven brewmaster. Of their many secret arts, brewing Brendle's Tears is the most closely guarded.

Megacosm – see *multiverse* or *macroverse.*

Men – the youngest and most prolific race of Ea'ae. Native flexibility and intuitiveness allows Men to excel in many fields, progressing quickly through their chosen arts.

Metamagics – the study of magic in and of itself, its laws, and governing principles.

Mithril – a particularly light, yet strong, magical metal.

Möerak – a skilled Dwarven miner with an uncanny ability to uncover valuable veins of ore, minerals, and gems.

Mulogo – accomplished wizard known for many magical theories and refinements as well as drafting *Mulogo's Treatise on Wizardry.*[2]

Scribe's note:

> 2. *A* cynical old curmudgeon who fancies himself something of a wizard.

Multimodal computational panlogic – the theory of structured and unstructured reasoning, rational and irrational decision-making, and generally making things up.

Multiverse – the entirety of multidimensional space, inclusive of alternate universes, planes, and dimensions. Also macroverse and megacosm.

Mysteries – a general name for types or classes of magic.

Nether realms – extradimensional planes home to infernals and other fiendish creatures. See *Abyss.*

New Unified Mental-Energetic Noesis – NUMEN. A synthetic Paratechnological being of great mental and physical capacity, able to take on many shapes, forms, and functions. An extension of the Paratechnology developed in the TAMERS units without need of an operator, as the NUMEN is guided by its own intelligence. Also, a play on words among Paratechnologists for their magical-technological creations that may one day supersede them.

Noeldri – literally, "flowing water". A Dwarven rune granting grace and agility both physically and mentally.

Noerlag[3] – a double-bladed great axe of high renown. Chosen weapon of Urdaen Doomhammer. Called *Fellblade* by the Dwarves. Called *Spinetickler* by the Orcs. Composer of texts of Dwarven lore. Of absolutely and most assuredly no relation to Duraeleon.

   Dwarf's Note:

   3. *A lyin' cur with a tongue as sharp as its treacherous blade.*

Noosphere – the realm of the mind, the collective consciousness, or the sphere of thought. A general name for the metamagical plane allowing for the shared existence and interaction both within and between various synthetic intelligences. A Paratechnological creation of the highest order. Also references the sphere of thought, mind, or knowledge itself. Also called the *Gnomosphere*.

Notional physics – the Paratechnological study of the higher (and lower) laws of the universe, the greater macroverse, and its various subsets.

Nüaerblun – literally, "dragon dung" in the tongue of the Dwarves. Often used as a Dwarven insult.

Nüaer'Daer – literally, "life's heart." A Dwarven term for dragons.

Nüaer'Duin – literally, "dragon fire" or "life's fire" in the tongue of the Dwarves. Among the Dwarves, dragon fire is respected for its magical properties and power so like the heat of Brendle's forge.

NUMEN – see *New Unified Mental-Energetic Noesis*.

Occlusion – a Paratechnologist known for his overzealous shaving habits.

Occlusion's razor – a simple axiom arrived at by Occlusion after much trial, error, and many, many cuts… getting the most for the least.

Oedenara – literally, "daemon's heart." A crystalline gem, found at the heart of some daemons, that has powerful magical properties and is of much practical use.

Omnicron – a Paratechnological device capable of generating and sustaining immersive, non-virtual actualities.

Omnispark – Gnomish conception of the ignited or expressed source of life unending, ever-changing and evolving, fueled by Phlogiston. *Deur Spricken Sprack* in Gnomish. Also called Yuan-chi, *magic*, *Aerya*, *Brendle's Spark*, and *the Light*, among other terms, by other races.

Orcs – a large and prolific evil race spread through the wilds and caverns of Ea'ae. Orcs are strong, aggressive, and full of guile, a race of warriors and shaman. Working in league with Trolls and Ogres, Orcs often lead their slower witted brethren on the field of battle.

Paladin – a holy warrior dedicated to and empowered by the Light. Paladins are vanquishers of evil, banishers of the unholy, adjudicators and arbiters, healers and almsmen. Many variants exist, some dedicated to particular deities and powerful entities, each with different talents, specialties, and ethos. The Dalaren Ka are one such group.

Parapsychology – the magical study of the mind, its features, moods, states, and manifestations.

Paratechnology – literally, "beyond technology." The study of making the imagined real and actualizing the impossible. The art and science of applied magic and magical technologies. Paratechnological apprehension is shared across many races, however the Gnomes' natural curiosity and creativity have brought Paratechnological expertise to its current refined state and have helped to spread its knowledge throughout the cosmos.

Phlogiston – called *Deur Spricken Sprack* in the tongue of Gnomes. In Gnomish reckoning, the invisible spark of life pervading the universe akin to an invisible metastate of gaseous energetic conductance. Once ignited, Phlogiston fuels all life as the Omnispark. When manipulated by will, the Phlogiston gives rise to magic. Also called Yuan-chi, *magic*, *Aerya*, *Brendle's Spark*, and *the Light*, among other terms, by other races and traditions.

Phylactery – an amulet, charm, or safeguard against harm or danger. Also, a vessel for relics.

Plane – one of many distinct layers of existence in the larger macro or multiverse. Often synonymous with universe or dimension.

Pocket dimension – a miniature space or reality created expressly for a specific purpose. In the case of the myriad pocket dimensions of Tellanon, these represent miniature universes intimately connected to Tellanon itself, extending its breadth and depth. More often, pocket dimensions are used to extend space within a given region—for example, to make the space within a bag or room larger.

Pocket fairy – small, often cantankerous fairies given to taking up residence in Gnomish pockets.

Powers – beings of great might, often extradimensional in origin.

Priest – one who has been accepted fully into the Order of the K'un Lun. See *Priest of K'un Lun*.

Priest of K'un Lun – an Order of mystics dedicated to the practice of various esoteric and martial traditions found nowhere else on Ea'ae. The way of the Priest is geared toward continual transformation and development within and without through the evolving practice of internal alchemy.

Priest of Maeth Onai – an order of magicians from the cold Northlands that practices a unique blend of mundane and divine magics whereby divine energies are channeled to perform traditional and inimitable spells.

Projection – a general term for a multi-dimensional representation of an object, such as a magical hologram or depiction. Also a reference to life-like, immersive news feeds displaying current happenings and items of worth.

Psion – a being gifted mentally and psychically.

Psionics – psychic mental powers and abilities as expressed by a psion.

Rakshasha – Sanskrit for demon. A race of powerful feline daemonic sorcerers in league with the Cabal.

Saedeus Moerdencanum – warlock, dictator, despot, and all-around not so nice guy. Saedeus's empire spread far and wide across several galaxies and planes through a pernicious combination of fell necromantic sorceries and high technologies. Saedeus's reign of intergalactic terror was ended when his conquests disrupted the vegetable supply of a particularly enterprising group of Gnomes with an inordinate fondness for rutabagas.

SAVERS – see *Self Actuated Variable Emergency Response System*.

Sceaduwulf – literally, "shadow wolf." A spectral wolf.

Schema – The patterning, diagramming, representation, and planning of Paratechnological devices, theorems, strategies, and abstractions.

Scierdyas – literally, "spectral dragons." Energetic beings very similar in appearance to dragons summoned from the unholy nether realms of the darkest abysms.

Self-Actuated Variable Emergency Response System – a Paratechnological clockwork emergency response bot of Gnomish invention, capable of independently responding to, assessing, and reacting to multiple life-threatening situations. Called *SAVERS* for short.

Sentry drones – a general name for Paratechnological defensive drones. See also *ARMED*.

Shade – a nebulous creature of Darkness.

Shadow – a general term for creatures of Darkness and their ilk. Those opposed to the energy of Life in all its manifestations and who seek to subvert, pervert, consume, or otherwise destroy the Light in all its manifold expressions.

Shadowkin – a general term for creatures of Darkness. See *Shadow*.

Shaur'Daus – literally, a "Stalker of Darkness" in the tongue of the Dracodaerans. Draconic warriors wreathed in the fires of heaven that do battle against the creatures of Darkness across the cosmos and beyond.

Shen Po – master of the void palm, one of the fallen founding fathers of the K'un Lun, member of the Cabal, and one time teacher of Master Wei.

Shiny – a highly sought after, much admired quality in Paratechnology. Shiny is a very complex term with many shades of meaning. Except when its meaning is simple. Typically understood as desirable or bright and highly reflective; or the state of being such. Discussions of shiny are never dull.

Skael – a people of nomadic traders who travel the skies in airships plying their wares.

Spreesprocket Goldpulley – Gnomish Paratechnologist and humble writer of many insightful texts.

Südaer – a Dwarven lorekeeper and magician.

Super sack – a magical Gnomish bottomless bag. Super sacks are often cluttered, disorganized, and very difficult to retrieve items from, especially within a short, highly critical period of time.

Suprachemistry – the study of how magical and nonmagical systems, compounds, elements, entities, and components interact, react, behave, change, and develop.

Synthetic intelligence – a Paratechnological term for the sentience resulting from the merger of two different intelligences. Typically, one intelligence is natural and the other is artificial, one is organic and the other is disembodied or a metamagical complex arising from technical sophistication, or one intelligence is formed explicitly to merge with and augment another. Far different from the Abstract and Construct's relationship with Citizens, for example, wherein one intelligence serves another directly and indirectly, synthetic intelligences are the result of a complete union between two disparate awarenesses, the resulting union having complete access to the knowledge and capabilities of both. Most typically, one intelligence is created explicitly to merge with and augment another, extending the field of sentient consciousness into directions and dimensions limited only by the imagination.

Also a reference to any created intelligence.

Taerris'thule – literally, "old home." Formerly a religious city and home to the seal of Eldre'gheu. Sometimes referred to as the City of the Fallen Gods.

TAMERS – see *Transmorphic Actionable Multidimensional Exo-Robotic System.*

Tellanon – literally, "Heaven's Landing" in the Old Tongue of Men. A spectacular floating island city in the sky, a center of commerce and diplomacy, and a starting point for both interstellar and interdimensional travel. Home of Illdrassil, the Home Guard, and Paratechnologists on Ea'ae.

Thane – traditional leader of a Dwarven clan.

Tinkerers – Paratechnologists focusing on clockwork devices melding magic and technology in forms often resembling complex mechanical devices. Most often associated with Gnomish Paratechnologists due to their strong imaginative mechanical tendencies.

Transmorphic Actionable Multidimensional Exo-Robotic System – A multi-functional, transforming exoarmor system created by Spreesprocket. Also known as TAMERS.

Traveling – teleportation or any other form of instantaneous travel ,whether inter- or intra-dimensional.

The Umbral Lord – see *the Enemy* or *Ur'Daus*.

Undermount – a general name for any Dwarven city or a Dwarven occupied region. Typically located in the bedrock beneath mountains. Undermounts are composed of Dwarven fastnesses and attendant halls and byways that grow within the roots of the hills. Also called delvings, though delvings are typically smaller in scale.

Ungar – literally, "earthen might". A Dwarven rune granting physical strength and endurance.

Urdaea – Urdaen's granddaughter.

Urdaen "Flamebeard" Doomhammer – Dwarven hero and inspiration for many a tome and tale. Most fortunate wielder of Noerlag.

Ur'Daena – literally, "the axe's lament." The uniquely Dwarven art of the axe. Many styles and forms are known, each generally ascribed to a specific family, clan, or thanedom. Variations in styles—from the use of great two-handed war axes taller than a man suited to the openness of the battlefield, to forms of double-bladed combat better suited to the close quarters of a mineshaft—are all practiced with distinctly Dwarven fervor.

When practiced by a master, a *Bor'Banna*, these styles rely as much on channeling the remnants of Brendle's original creation magic through the axe as they do on physical prowess for their efficacy. When wielded by a true master, the axe of the *Bor'Banna* is said to glow with the light and heat of Brendle's original forge.

Ur'Daus – literally, "The Darkness." Also known as the Enemy, the Creeping Shadow, the Devourer of Worlds, the Umbral Lord, the Great Devourer, and many others. A fathomless Light consuming Darkness trapped between dimensions in Ages long past.

Vanduen – literally, "divine regeneration". A Dwarven *Karaduen* that enhances healing capacities, speeding recovery and repair from exhaustion and injury.

Vöer – troll, in the tongue of the Dwarves.

Vöerdan – literally, "Troll saliva or spittle." A Dwarven insult.

Void – the wellspring of creation. The limitless potential underlying all existence.

Vradek – Orcish gruel made from ground bones simmered in blood.

Vyaera – literally, "wanderers along the path." An Elven term for those sharing the same path, quest, purpose, or journey.

War of Shadows – one name for the first war with the Cabal and their dark allies, waged on Ea'ae in the distant past.

Worgs – massive wolves used by Orcs as mounts in lieu of horses.

Wyrm – an ancient or powerful dragon.

Yerens – a noble race of yeti-like creatures. Singers of the worldsong. Called the Shapers of the True Song, Shapers, and Singers.

Younglings – a common name for Dwarven children.

Yuan-chi – the primordial energy, the inherent unrealized potential, of the universe; the celestial or divine *chi*.

About the Author

Joe is currently a minor underhenchman in a vast underground network of informants, spies, revolutionaries, thugs, hirelings, bosses, villains, assassins, myriad accomplices, and other people you probably don't want to meet.

Including influences such as Shunryu Suzuki, Tolkien, Krishnamurti, Iain M. Banks, Laozi, Stephen R. Donaldson, Philip Kapleau, Raymond E. Feist, Edward O. Wilson, Dan Simmons, and David Bohm, Joe creates existential fantasy filled with rich worlds, concepts, stories, and ideas.

Joe holds an advanced degree in environmental management from Duke University where he also studied religion with a focus on meditative, experiential, and transformative traditions. Additionally, Joe graduated with (dubious) honors from the Tellanon Institute of Noetic Knowledge, Education, and Research (TINKER) and has yet to put this knowledge to good use.

When not at play with his family, he enjoys reading, writing, and relaxation. When he can, Joe also practices various martial traditions in which he has attained the victim level of proficiency.

In addition to *Nemesis*, Joe is also the author of the *Chronicles of the Fists* trilogy, *Everygnome's Guide to Paratechnology*, *Confessions of an Angry Dwarf*, and *Mulogo's Treatise on Wizardry*. He is also working on something else but really cannot say more on the matter at present.

Author's Final Note[1]

I hope you enjoyed reading this book as much as I did writing it.

Whether these words transported you to another place, one you enjoyed wholeheartedly, or pushed you away without lasting impression, I would welcome your fair and honest review (good, bad, or indifferent) of my book wherever you may choose.

If you truly did appreciate this book, feel free to spread the word to your friends, family, and random acquaintances. I would also love for you to visit me at either my website at www.josephjbailey.com or on my Facebook Author's Page.

If you would like to learn about future book releases, please consider signing up for my book announcement newsletter.

Many thanks and happy reading!

Joseph J. Bailey

Read this if you value your life:

1. *You've probably had enough of these.*

www.ingramcontent.com/pod-product-compliance
Lightning Source LLC
Chambersburg PA
CBHW031844170626
46807CB00004B/1612